THANK YOU!

Your purchase of this very special book
supports our mission of educating children
about the importance of preserving our world.
A percentage of our sales will be used to
support global conservation.
To find out more, please visit us at
www.barefootbooks.com

For my sister, Liz — C. C.

Barefoot Books
124 Walcot Street
Bath, BA1 5BG, UK

Barefoot Books
2067 Massachusetts Ave
Cambridge, MA 02140, USA

First published in Great Britain by Barefoot Books, Ltd
and in the United States of America by Barefoot Books, Inc. in 2007

Illustrations copyright © 2007 by Christopher Corr
The moral right of Christopher Corr to be identified as the
illustrator of this work has been asserted

This book has been printed on 100% acid-free paper

Graphic design by Penny Lamprell, Lymington, England
Reproduction by Grafiscan, Verona
Printed and bound in China by PrintPlus Ltd

This book was typeset in Kosmik and ChildsPlay
The illustrations were prepared in gouache on Fabriano paper

Hardback ISBN 978-1-84686-043-0

British Cataloguing-in-Publication Data:
a catalogue record for this book is available from the British Library

57986

Library of Congress Cataloging-in-Publication Data

Corr, Christopher.
    Whole world / Christopher Corr.
      p. cm.
    Summary: An illustrated version of the well-known song, featuring the relationship between people
and the natural world.
    ISBN-13: 978-1-84686-043-0 (hardcover : alk. paper)
    1. Spirituals (Songs)—Texts. 2. Children's songs, English—United States—Texts.
[1. Spirituals (Songs) 2. Songs.]   I. He's got the whole world in his hands. II. Title.
    PZ8.3.C81882Who 2007
    782.42—dc22
    [E]
                                        2006023455

WHOLE WORLD

Illustrated by Christopher Corr
Sung by Fred Penner

Barefoot Books
Celebrating Art and Story

We've got the whole world in our hands,
We've got the whole world in our hands,

We've got the whole world in our hands,
We've got the whole world in our hands!

She's got the sun and the moon in her hands,

She's got the whole world in her hands!

He's got the mountains and the valleys in his hands,
He's got the mountains and the valleys in his hands,

He's got the mountains and the valleys in his hands,
He's got the whole world in his hands!

She's got the plains and the deserts in her hands,

She's got the plains and the deserts in her hands,

She's got the plains and the deserts in her hands,
She's got the whole world in her hands!

He's got the lakes and the rivers in his hands,
He's got the lakes and the rivers in his hands,

He's got the lakes and the rivers in his hands,
He's got the whole world in his hands!

She's got the trees and the flowers in her hands,
She's got the trees and the flowers in her hands,

She's got the trees and the flowers in her hands,
She's got the whole world in her hands!

She's got the fish of the sea in her hands,

She's got the fish of the sea in her hands,

She's got the fish of the sea in her hands,

She's got the whole world in her hands!

He's got the towns and the cities in his hands,
He's got the whole world in his hands!

We've got the whole world in our hands,
We've got the whole world in our hands,

We've got the whole world in our hands,
We've got the whole world in our hands!

Did You Know?

We really do have the whole world in our hands — it is up to us to take care of it!

Here is some information about the creatures and environments in this book:

Sun

Almost all of the earth's energy comes from the sun — without the sun, the earth would be a big block of ice! People have depended on the sun for as long as there has been life on earth, for lots of different reasons. The sun has always been very important to farmers, because the crops need its light. In ancient times, the movements of the sun were used for telling the time and setting apart the different seasons.

Moon

The moon is at its brightest in our night sky, after the sun has set. Farmers and gardeners often depend on the moon to know when to plant new seeds, and ocean tides are controlled by the pull of the moon. There are lots of moon festivals all over the world, where people celebrate its wonder. Air pollution is changing our view of the moon — smog makes the sky look thick, foggy and dark, which blocks the moon from our sight.

Mountains

The great mountain ranges of the world were created millions of years ago by pressure caused when tectonic plates — sections of the earth's surface — pushed up against each other. Mountains have historically formed natural boundaries between different countries because they are difficult or impossible to pass, especially in winter. Many mountains that have been snow-capped for centuries are now changing, as global warming raises temperatures and the snowcaps melt.

Valleys

Valleys are the lowlands between mountains. Many of the world's valleys were created at the end of the Ice Age, when the glaciers melted. Valleys often have very rich soil, so they are areas where farming communities have regularly settled. In just a spoonful of this soil, there can be a billion living things, such as worms and seeds. Valleys also offer protection from severe weather, and are used as trading routes.

Plains

Plains are large areas of flat, open land, such as savannahs and tundra. Animals like cheetahs and zebras live on savannahs, while, in fertile areas, plains are used for farming. Plains exist all over the world, from North America to Spain to Iran, but many of them are becoming polluted. As rain falls and trickles down the land, it picks up any pollutants as it goes. These then settle in the low plains.

Deserts

Deserts are dry lands, and can be either very hot or very cold. Some deserts have no rain for years and years! Deserts may seem like places without life, but lots of living things make their homes there, such as bats, birds, frogs, lizards, plants, snakes and even fish. The lives of these plants and animals are all connected — they depend on each other for survival.

Lakes

Lakes are very important to the environment: lakes supply drinking water, make electricity, and provide water for fields. Lakes are also ecosystems, or communities, of plants and animals. As our environment changes, the natural ecosystems do too. For example, tiny creatures called plankton live in lakes. The other fish and mammals depend on the plankton for food. As lakes heat up because of global warming, the plankton suffer because they live near the hot surface. If these tiny creatures die, so does the entire ecosystem of the lake.

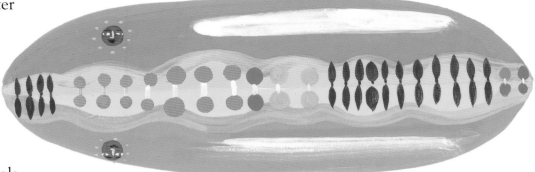

Rivers

A river is a natural stream of water that is bigger than a brook or creek. Historically, rivers have determined where cities are built and where trade routes are developed. Lots of wildlife make their home in rivers, like fish, water rats and ducks. Almost all rivers empty out into the ocean, bringing with them a lot of rain. Therefore, pollution of rivers harms not only the river itself, but also the oceans and all the creatures that live there.

Trees

There are many, many kinds of trees in the world. Trees are beautiful, but they are also very important for many reasons. Trees provide oxygen and moisture, and remove carbon dioxide to make the air cleaner. They absorb water to prevent flooding, and many animals, insects and birds make their homes in trees. Trees provide fruit to feed us and leafy branches to shade us. Where would we be without trees?

Flowers

Flowers come in all shapes and sizes. They are bright in order to attract insects and birds to their blossoms. The flowers provide nectar to drink, and in return the insects and birds carry pollen and seeds from flower to flower, fertilizing them and spreading them to new areas so that more flowers can grow.

In recent years, pesticides used on industrialized farms have destroyed many varieties of flower. If more flowers die, many more insects and birds who depend on them for food will also disappear.

Birds

There are almost countless species of birds in the world, and they all play a very important role in the environment. Birds eat rodents, insects and other pests — up to half their weight every day! They pollinate flowers and spread plant seeds so that plants grow back each year. And can you imagine a world without birds singing?

Fish

There are tens of thousands of kinds of fish on earth. Fish live in almost all the waters of the world, including rivers, lakes, oceans and ponds. As the temperature of the earth begins to rise, so does the temperature of these bodies of water where fish make their home. This could become a big problem, as fish like trout and salmon need cool waters to survive.

Towns and Cities

There are different kinds of towns and cities all over the world. They usually spring up because of trading needs. Many towns and cities are on the coast, while others are on rivers or inland, forming trading places for local communities. Nowadays, these communities can exist for all kinds of reasons: they may serve local farmers, manufacturing industries such as car production, scientific research laboratories, or service industries such as tourism. Prosperous cities have always attracted people to them, and the busiest ones draw people from all over the world. Because there are so many people, buildings and cars in cities, there are also problems with pollution and with waste management. Our cities use many of the earth's resources and produce a lot of waste. The way we treat our cities today will affect all future generations.

Ways to Reduce Global Warming

Global warming is caused by carbon dioxide that is released into the atmosphere. There are lots of different causes for this, such as cars and planes. Global warming causes temperature and climate changes that affect every living thing on earth. There are some simple things that everyone can do to help reduce global warming:

- Don't fly or drive if you don't have to. Take the bus or the train, walk, run or cycle!

- Use renewable energy — that means power from wind or solar energy, from the sun.

- Recycle! This dramatically reduces the amount of waste in our environment.

- Use less hot water. It takes a lot of energy to heat up water.

- Turn off and unplug your TV, stereo and computer when you're not using them.

- Hang your clothes outside to dry instead of using the tumble dryer.

- Use recycled paper to save trees from being cut down.

- Eat less meat. Forests full of trees that reduce carbon dioxide in the air are cut down to make way for cows that will be used for food.

- Buy local and organic food. This means less fuel is being used to transport the food to you.

- Replace old light bulbs with compact fluorescent bulbs — these use 60 per cent less energy than regular bulbs.

- Plant a tree — it will absorb one ton of carbon dioxide in its lifetime.

Sing Along

The original version of this song was written by African American pianist and composer, Margaret Bonds (1913-1972). "He's Got the Whole World in His Hands" is very well known as a gospel spiritual.

We've got the whole world _____ in our_ hands, We've got the whole_ world _____

in our_ hands, We've got the whole world _____ in our_ hands, We've got the whole world in our hands! _____

She's got the sun and the moon in her hands . . .

He's got the mountains and the valleys in his hands . . .

She's got the plains and the deserts in her hands . . .

He's got the lakes and the rivers in his hands . . .

She's got the trees and the flowers in her hands . . .

He's got the birds of the air in his hands . . .

She's got the fish of the sea in her hands . . .

He's got the towns and the cities in his hands . . .

Repeat first verse!

Barefoot Books
Celebrating Art and Story

At Barefoot Books, we celebrate art and story that opens
the hearts and minds of children from all walks of life, inspiring
them to read deeper, search further, and explore their own creative gifts.
Taking our inspiration from many different cultures, we focus on themes
that encourage independence of spirit, enthusiasm for learning, and sharing of
the world's diversity. Interactive, playful and beautiful, our products
combine the best of the present with the best of the past to
educate our children as the caretakers of tomorrow.

Live Barefoot!
Join us at **www.barefootbooks.com**